D0522198

By Melissa Lagonegro
Illustrated by Pulsar Estudio

First published by Parragon in 2012
Parragon
Queen Street House
4 Queen Street
Bath BA1 1HE, UK
www.parragon.com

ISBN 978-1-4454-4744-5

Printed in China

A Dream for a Princess

A little story for little learners

Bath • New York • Singapore • Hong Kong • Cologne • Delhi
Melbourne • Amsterdam • Johannesburg • Auckland • Shenzhen

There once was a girl
named Cinderella.
She was kind and gentle.

Cinderella lived with
her wicked stepmother
and stepsisters.

She had many chores.

She served them tea.

She cooked their food.

She washed their clothes.

One day,
a letter came
from the palace.
"Come meet the Prince
at a Royal Ball," it said.

The stepsisters
were very excited.
Cinderella was, too!

Cinderella dreamed of wearing a fancy gown...

...and dancing with

the Prince.

Cinderella's stepmother
gave her more chores.
Cinderella did not have
time to make her
ball gown.

"Surprise!"
cried her little friends.
They had made her
a fancy gown.

"Now I can go
to the ball!"
cheered Cinderella.

Oh, no!
The stepsisters
tore her gown.
It was ruined!

Cinderella cried.

Piff, puff, poof!
Her Fairy Godmother
appeared.

"You cannot go
to the ball
like that," she said.

She waved
her magic wand.
Poof!

A royal coach.

White horses.

Two coachmen.

And a beautiful gown!

Cinderella was going
to the ball!

At the ball,
the Prince saw
Cinderella.

"May I have this dance?" he asked.

Cinderella was so happy.
She was wearing
a fancy gown.

And she was dancing
with the Prince!